The Mainland

OBAN
TIMES
GET
YOUR COPY
HERE

ISLE of STRUAY
SHOP & POST OFFICE

BISTRO

PIER

WEST
HIGHLAND
FREE PRESS
ORDER
NOW

WELC

The Shop & Post Office

BY THE SAME AUTHOR

Katie Morag and the Two Grandmothers
Katie Morag Delivers the Mail
Katie Morag and the Big Boy Cousins
Katie Morag and the Tiresome Ted
Katie Morag and the New Pier
Peedie Peebles' Summer or Winter Book
Peedie Peebles' Colour Book

1 3 5 7 9 10 8 6 4 2

Copyright © Mairi Hedderwick 1995

Mairi Hedderwick has asserted her right
under the Copyright, Designs and Patents
Act, 1988 to be identified as the author
and illustrator of this work

First published in the United Kingdom
1995
by the Bodley Head Children's Books
Random House, 20 Vauxhall Bridge
Road, London SW1V 2SA

Random House Australia (Pty) Limited
20 Alfred Street, Milsons Point, Sydney,
New South Wales 2061, Australia

Random House New Zealand Limited
18 Poland Road, Glenfield,
Auckland 10, New Zealand

Random House South Africa (Pty) Limited
PO Box 337, Bergvlei 2012, South Africa

Random House UK Limited Reg. No.
954009

A CIP catalogue record for this book is
available from the British Library

ISBN 0 370 31977X

Typeset by S.X. Composing Ltd.,
Rayleigh, Essex

Printed in China

For the Flautist

KATIE MORAG AND THE WEDDING

Mairi Hedderwick

wedding invitation
The Pleasure of the Company of
The McColls
is requested

THE BODLEY HEAD

London

Ever since the new pier had been built on the Isle of Struay, Granma Mainland visited regularly.

Katie Morag McColl was delighted to see more of her other grandmother. But most delighted of all the islanders was Neilly Beag. He fancied Granma Mainland and always looked so sad when she went away. Then he would write lots of long letters to her in the city on the mainland and wait impatiently for the mailboat to bring back a reply.

This kept Mrs McColl, the Postmistress, very busy. Everyone on the island said a romance was afoot.

"Maybe even a wedding!" whispered the Ferryman's wife in between serving teas to the visitors.

"Pah! A wedding? I'll believe it when I see it!" muttered Grannie Island when she heard the gossip.

Katie Morag was very excited at the thought of a wedding. It usually meant a big party; it also meant that the two people getting married wanted to live together instead of far apart.

Would Granma Mainland come to live in Neilly Beag's house on the island? That would be lovely! But, oh dear, what if Neilly went to live with Granma Mainland in the far away city?

"If there is a wedding will Neilly Beag be our Grandad?" Katie Morag asked when she and Liam arrived at Grannie Island's, just in time for dinner.

Her Grannie did not answer.

"Wheesht! Go sit at the table!" she frowned instead.

"We've got two grandmothers. Why don't we have two grandfathers?"

"Wheesht! Will you SIT DOWN!" glared Grannie Island.

It was a long time since Katie Morag had seen such a glower in Grannie Island's eye. It was time to stop asking questions.

OLD PHOTOS

As Katie Morag pushed Liam homewards she wondered why Grannie Island was in such a bad mood. It made her feel sad.

When they got to the village Neilly Beag was at his front door. He had a huge pile of stamped addressed envelopes in his arms.

"The invitations for the wedding!" he beamed proudly. "Can you take them to the Post Office, Katie Morag?"

That cheered Katie Morag up no end.

"Can *we* go? Can *we* go?" chorused Katie Morag and Liam when the silver and gold invitation was put on the mantelpiece.

"Of course!" smiled Mr and Mrs McColl. "*Everyone* will be going to the wedding!"

"And the new baby?"

"Of course . . ."

"And the Ferryman and his wife . . . and the Lady Artist . . . and the new teacher?"

"Of course! Of course!" laughed Mr and Mrs McColl.

"And Grannie Island?" asked Katie Morag.

Suddenly everything went very quiet in the McColl kitchen. Grown ups can be very strange thought Katie Morag, sometimes they answer questions and sometimes they do not . . .

That night in bed Katie Morag complained to Liam.

"If we didn't answer when we were asked questions we would be called rude."

"Rood!" agreed Liam.

KATIE MORAG & THE NEW PIER
KATIE MORAG & THE BIG BOY COUSINS
KATIE MORAG & THE TIRESOME TED
KATIE MORAG & THE TWO GRANDMOTHERS
KATIE MORAG DELIVERS THE MAIL

MAY

M T W T F S Sun

"Granma Mainland always answers questions. I am going to write her a letter," declared Katie Morag.

This is what the letter said:

Me

THE SHOP AND POST OFFICE
ISLE OF STRUAY
Proprietors:
Jean and Peter Nicol McColl

May 27

Dear Granma Manelan,
we are looking fowad to yur
wedding. ← me ← Liam
Grannie Eyelan is verry
cross. Can you find her a
Gandad too plese ?
lots of luv and
Katie Morag XXXXXx

PS Liam hops you and Neilly hav
lots of babbies

Peedie Peebles
COLOUR BOOK

The next few weeks on the island were very busy.

All sorts of parcels and crates came off the boat and were carried up to Neilly's house or to the Village Hall.

Neilly dieted so much Mrs McColl had to get a needle and thread to alter his smart new suit. The Ferryman's wife made a giant of a chocolate cake; she and Mr McColl had to stand on stools to decorate it.

BULK
ICING
SUGAR

COCOA

Katie Morag and Liam made a special present for the bride and groom. The new baby lent ribbons for flags. Liam thought it was Christmas. He kept chanting "Anta Claws! Anta Claws!" and even hung up his stocking. Katie Morag waited for a reply from Granma Mainland.

The day of the wedding drew near.

Granma Mainland and all the relatives and friends were due to arrive on the boat the day before the big event.

Nobody had seen Grannie Island for days.

I'VE FOUND HIM!

All the islanders went to the pier to meet the guests arriving off the boat, but there was *no* sign of Granma Mainland. Neilly Beag was just about to burst into tears when a loud clattering and whirring reverberated around Village Bay.

It was a helicopter and Granma Mainland was right in the front with the white bearded pilot.

"Anta Claws!" yelled Liam.

"It isn't Santa Claus, silly!" cried Katie Morag. *She* knew who it was.

Grandad Island swung Katie Morag up in the air. "Last time I saw you, Katie Morag, you were just a sparkle in your mum and dad's eyes!"

Katie Morag and Liam raced Grandad Island up to the Village Hall to help with the decorations for the wedding party.

Grandad Island asked if Grannie Island was going to the wedding.

"You'd better go and find out for yourself," said Granma Mainland, somewhat sternly.

STRUAY
VILLAGE HALL

KEY AT MRS. BAYVIEW'S
ALWAYS
PLEASE / RETURN

FLY

ME

Katie Morag watched Grandad Island set off on the long walk round to Grannie Island's house, on the other side of the bay. She worried that the fierce glare in Grannie Island's eye of late would frighten him away.

The Wedding Menu

OBSTER CLAW SOUP
OR
STUFFED TURNIP
~
AGGIS BURGERS
OR
ARROT STEAKS
~
CHIPS
~
CAKE & ICECREAM

Katie Morag need not have worried.

On the day of the wedding nobody's eyes were glaring – everyone's eyes were sparkling, especially the two grandads'. But Grannie Island's and Granma Mainland's were the brightest and sparkliest eyes of all.

Granma Mainland and Neilly Beag were to honeymoon on the neighbouring island of Fuay. There were no people on Fuay, only sheep, and they all belonged to Neilly.

"And all the lambs next spring will be yours, Mrs Beag, my wee Bobby Dazzler!"

Liam was right. Granma Mainland *was* going to have lots of babies to look after.

GOOD LUCK

Sheep Dip

JUST MARRIED

HASTE YE BACK

But Granma Mainland was not going to give up her flat in the city. She and Neilly would commute between Struay, Fuay and the mainland. And Katie Morag could visit whenever she wanted.

It took a lot of persuading to get Grannie Island up in the helicopter.
Grannie Island did not like travelling.

Grandad Island loved travelling and never stayed in one place for long.

"East, West, Home's Best!" insisted Grannie Island, clinging to her
seat like a limpet.

Katie Morag knew then, that Grandad Island would be leaving soon.
"Grandad, when you go travelling can I come too sometimes?"
"Certainly, Katie Morag – anywhere in the world."
Katie Morag was thrilled. She looked forward to visiting Fuay, the city
on the mainland and now, anywhere in the world!
But it was good to know that Grannie Island would always be there on
the Island of Struay when she got back home.